i

THE CONGRESSMAN

DON ALLEN

ISBN: 979-8-9883175-6-2

eISBN: 979-8-9883175-7-9

Publisher: Don Allen

Also, by Don Allen

Sean Murphy Series
Satisfaction
Chaos
The Launderer
The Brotherhood
The Developer
Treasure
Stolen Wealth

George Basdakis Series
Check for Junk
The Gurkha

Sam Goodwin Series
Dog Walker
The Irishmen
The Congressman

1 Minding My Own Business

Our lives were returning to normal. Carol's books were doing well. The Boston Literary Society sponsored her at several book readings over the summer. My workload at the *Salt 'n Pepper Detective Agency* had decreased considerably since we helped MI-6 eliminate an IRA threat. And Maxi was content to romp with Muffy, Fenk Ciziri's poodle, when Fenk accompanied Carol on her morning walks in the park. All was well in West Roxbury.

I made it a practice to visit the Detective Agency a few times a week. Occasionally there was some activity, a new client needing dirt on his/her spouse, a politician trying to head off some pending scandal, or money missing from the till.

"Where's Maxi this morning?" asked Rossie. Rossie was named after Sister Rosetta Tharpe, a famous gospel singer. She is our part-time receptionist when not attending acting classes at Emerson College's School of Theater. She is also Jimmy's niece. Jimmy is the Pepper in the '*Salt 'n Pepper*,' a co-founder of the Agency and a retired Boston Police Detective. As a former college lineman, he brought a certain level of 'physical presence' to the Detective Agency.

"She's home being pampered by Carol."

Is Danny in?" Danny is the other half of the '*Salt 'n Pepper*.' Danny O'Kaye is a wiry little Irishman, pale skin, blond hair, blue eyes, and subject to frequent sunburns. He's also a retired Boston Police Detective.

To round out the team, I am Samuel Goodwin, also retired from the Boston Police Department where I was a dog handler. Maxi, my eighty-pound German Shepherd, considered too old for continued service, retired with me.

"Danny's in his office talking with a potential client. He said you should go in when you got here," Rossie said.

Entering the office, I found Danny in a heated discussion with an elderly man while a middle-aged lady looked on. Seeing me, he breaks off, "Sam, I'm glad you're here. This is Mr. Plumbtree and Ms. Handson. They are with the local Democrat National Committee. They want us to find dirt they can use for a malfeasance charge against one of their incumbents. I'm just telling Mr. Plumbtree that we are not into muckraking. For that, they should contact the Boston Globe.

"Mr. Goodwin, isn't it," said Ms. Handson. "The incumbent we are targeting has become a laughingstock in Washington. She will probably lose the next election, so we are just trying to get her to resign peacefully."

"I agree with Danny; your best bet is to talk with newspaper reporters and build a case with them. That's what they do."

"I don't want to get involved with politicians," Danny said after they left. "They will lie to your face and then tell you it was your fault for believing them."

"Is Jimmy in today?" I asked.

"No, he's hustling business from your favorite politician, Mayor O'Brien. Her niece is planning an event that Her Honor feels some security may be required. Jimmy is meeting with the Mayor's niece to get details."

"And what's wrong with the police?"

"It's a private event, and O'Brien doesn't want to appear to be misusing city resources. So, she turned to us. She did make one request; she wants Maxi there."

2 The Party

The following Friday evening, Eillen Nelson, the Mayor's niece, held a small gathering, a hundred fifty-plus people, a shakedown for donations to her favorite charity, the DNC. Danny and Jimmy were tasked with mingling with the crowd. Their main function was to quietly remove anyone who got too rambunctious. My task, with Maxi, was to patrol the perimeter to catch any unwelcome guests.

Among the fashionably late arrivals were Mr. Plumbtree and Ms. Handson. As they entered the grounds, they saw me. "Sam, Sam Goodwin, isn't it? And this must be Maxi," Plumbtree said as he stepped back. "I'm surprised to see you here. I thought the *Salt 'n Pepper Detective Agency* avoided politics."

"We try to, but Maxi and the Mayor have a history. As a favor to her, we agreed to provide security services for her niece."

As the two proceeded up the driveway, one of the caterers was pushing a trolly cart of party-size sandwiches into the catering tent. Maxi caught a whiff of the salmon pâté and was momentarily distracted. The young lady pushing the trolly looked at me, looked at Maxi, and asked, "Would she like a small piece?"

Maxi had a new friend.

The evening proceeded with no mishaps other than Jimmy escorting one of the older Party bosses into the house for a 'sit-down.'

4

The old man had had a few too many and was making inappropriate comments to the female waitstaff.

Mayor O'Brien found me leaning against a tree on the edge of the grounds with Maxi sitting beside me. "Maxi, who's a good girl tonight?" she said as she walked up.

"You and Maxi have had some excitement since you both retired. It seems I read about the two of you at least once a month."

"I feel as if I've had more action since I retired; perhaps I should rejoin the force for some downtime," I jokingly replied.

The Mayor and I, and Maxi, go back several years. Maxi and I found a kidnapped child and apprehended the kidnapper. It was a big case at the time. The child was missing for several days, and a huge ransom was demanded. While suffering stitches from Maxi's takedown, the kidnapper was sentenced to thirty years at Walpole. Maxi and I received high praise from Her Honor at the time.

"Sam, you ever think about running for office? I understand the 7th Congressional District may be open this year," the Mayor said. "You have many followers out there. Should I ask Mr. Plumbtree to call you?"

"No, I'm not cut out for politics, and besides, I think 'Salt 'n Pepper' alienated Mr. Plumbtree when Danny turned him down last week. But thank you for thinking of me."

3 A Nudge

A month later Carol and I were walking around the pond in the park at the end of our street. The idyllic setting reminded me of Mr. Wilkins's encounter with three punks, the same three who later attempted to rob me. After I pointed out that they could not outrun Maxi, they agreed to sit meekly on the bench and wait for the patrol car.

As we rounded the back side of the pond, we found Fenk sitting on one of the park benches. Fenk Ciziri is an Iraq refugee; more specifically, she is an ethnic Yazidi. She is in her early fifties, and one of the few women admitted to the University of Bagdad under Saddam Hussain, where she earned her medical degree. After ISIS captured her homeland in northern Iraq she escaped to a refugee camp run by a Christian aid group in Turkey. From there, she made her way to an Iraqi resettlement group in Boston. Being somewhat fluent in English, she continued to work with that group as an interpreter.

She was targeted by *The Islamic Society of Boston* after identifying one of their members as the former manager of the ISIS rape hotel in Mossel. A jihadi was sent to kill her. Maxi heard Muffy barking; she alerted me, and we saved Fenk. Okay, the story was a bit more involved, but that is the gist of it.

As I said, we found her on the park bench, Muffy at her feet. She was clearly distressed. Carol sat beside her and asked what the problem was.

"The Government is threatening to close the Refugee Center and relocate my people to temporary shelters on a military base. Many of our people have been here for several years and have established roots. Homeland Security wants us out of the way so they can house immigrants and the homeless. They claim we are just refugees and will be returning to our homeland soon."

"They can't do that!" Carol exclaimed.

"That's not right; it must just be a misunderstanding," I said. "I'll talk to the Mayor to get this cleared up."

The following morning I was at city hall when it opened to the public. I made a beeline to the Mayor's suite of offices and requested a meeting with the Mayor.

"Sam," a voice said behind me. Turning. I was face-to-face with Mayor O'Brien. "Come into my office, and we can talk. Bernice, see if our guest would like some coffee."

I passed on Bernice's offer of refreshments and launched into the reason for my visit, the proposed relocation of the Iraq refugees.

"Mayor O'Brien, you recall the Islamic terrorist threats we faced shortly after I retired. The Iraq refugees were key players in helping resolve that threat. Now the Feds are proposing to relocate them. That's not right."

"I agree and have been fighting the idea for several months. But this is a federal action that Homeland Security initiated. I can get some sympathy, but I don't have the clout needed to turn this off."

"Who does?"

"Well, you could. Remember I mentioned the 7th Congressional District is open and the DNC is looking for electable candidates.

You'd be a shoo-in. If you ran in the primary, which by the way, time is getting short for newcomers to enter, I'd campaign for you."

"But I'm not interested in political office," I said.

"That's a shame; you'd make an excellent congressman. If you want to help your neighbor, think about it. I'm going to give your name to Mr. Plumbtree. If you change your mind, call him at this number. Next Wednesday is the cutoff date for the primary registrations."

***

"Carol, should I run for Congress? Mayor O'Brien is telling me that is the only way I can help Fenk."

After an initial burst of laughter, "You, a congressman? You'd be better than most of the idiots in Washington."

"I have until Wednesday to make my mind up."

That afternoon I asked Danny and Jimmy the same question.

"You have the Mayor's support," said Danny, "go for it. You may never get the chance again."

"Go for what?" asked Rossie as she entered the office with the day's mail.

"Run for Congress," said Jimmy.

"For the seat the twit is being forced out of? Hell yes, go for it," said Rossie.

"Well, I guess it's decided," I said. "I can get at least five votes, you three, Carol, and mine."

I pulled out the card the Mayor gave me with Plumbtree's number and had almost finished placing my call, "You are all sure about this?" I asked as I punched in the last number.

4 Campaign

Ms. Handson took charge of my campaign. "After you make it through the primaries, you will have no problem in the general election," said Ruth Handson. "With the Mayor's support, you are a shoo-in. And the pièce de résistance will be Maxi on the stage with you. She has a respectable following with both dog lovers and 'law and order' types."

The general election was in November. The primary was in August when Party dilettantes were on vacation. Three debates were scheduled, the first in late July. I had two opponents. The first was a twenty-six-year-old, gender-neutral radical from Cambridge named Epsy. He/she supported free abortions, open borders, and the elimination of the military. The second, my only real challenger was Mildred Coming, an independent and wealthy sixty-six-year-old lady who was a perpetual candidate. Her focus was on issues that support family values. She normally drew a respectable number of votes but never enough to win.

Mildred was the first to speak at the July debate. I followed with my opening remarks, receiving cheers at all the right points. Maxi was sitting at my side, tail wagging.

Epsy jumped to the podium before I could return to my seat and started with remarks about my prop. "How can you trust a man who needs a dog to make his case?" he yelled, pointing at Maxi. As if on cue, Maxi's fur bristled, and a low-throated growl could be heard emanating behind her bared canines. Epsy got the largest audience reaction that day as he/she turned in panic and fell off the stage to the applause and laughter of the crowd.

The next two debates were anticlimactic. Epsy dropped out after the second debate, and Mildred and I forged a bond. She knew she wouldn't win but wanted to keep family issues alive. That was why she ran every two years. I committed myself to supporting a couple of her causes.

I received 81 percent of the primary vote.

We were in Boston, in Massachusetts, and the Republicans fielded a candidate in the 7th District more for appearances than anything else. The GOP candidate was looking to get some name recognition for next year's school board race. CNN announced my victory moments after the polls closed.

5 Mr. Goodwin Goes to Washinton

Ms. Handson took charge of my victory celebration. She reserved the Durgin-Park restaurant for a private party. Mildred, a gracious loser, funded the celebration.

As the guest of honor, I was expected to say a few words to all my supporters. I was surprised to see the number of people who turned out. Sargent O'Brian, my former commander at the police kennel, pretty much summed it all up when he loudly turned to me and said, "You know it was Maxi that got you here!" To the applause of the crowd, I took the MC's mike responding, "And I expect to be with her when we enter the House chamber in January – someone has to cast her vote."

"On a more serious note, I'd like to thank everyone here for your support. The reason I got into this race was Fenk Ciziri. Fenk, can you come up here, please?" You could tell she was not eager to come to the front, but she did.

With Fenk beside me, I told her story. "The Government is threatening to close the Iraqi Refugee Center and relocate her people to temporary shelters on a military base. Homeland Security wants the refugees out of the way so they can house undocumented immigrants. DHS claims Iraqi refugees will be repatriated ... even though most have been here for many years and have put down roots. This is not right, and as Mayor O'Brien pointed out, if I want to fight this, I have to be on the inside."

"Welcome to the House," said the would be Speaker, George Mansfield. "The business before us today is to get you all, all four hundred thirty-five voting members, sworn in so we can elect the Speaker of the House. I see Party leaders have most of you sitting with your Party. One or two freshmen appear to have wandered to the wrong side of the aisle. I hope that's not indicative of how you plan to vote."

After a little shuffling of seats, "The vote for Speaker is scheduled for the end of the week," he said. "There are two hundred nineteen Democrats and two hundred sixteen Republicans, a difference of three votes. This is the most balanced Congress I have ever seen. It's going to be an interesting two years."

Before adjourning, Mansfield launched into a brief review of the traditions of the House, the do's and the don'ts, and explaining specific rules would be established later after the House Speaker is selected. He concluded his speech with, "We will all meet back here at ten in the morning this Friday to vote for Speaker."

"Would all Democratic members please remain behind so we can have a little chat?" said Representative Mansfield.

Two hundred nineteen Democrats and six nonvoting members remained in the well of the House as the Republicans filed out.

"I see we have six new members. You, Mr. Goodman, please remember to sit to the left of the aisle with your fellow members. With such a narrow margin, we don't want to suggest a weakness in our ranks."

"As you all know, the former Speaker has endorsed me for Speaker, as have several ranking members. Is there any objection? Are any other names being put forward for consideration? If not, I have a proposed list of committee assignments for your consideration.

As has been our practice, assignments can be swapped during our first thirty days. After that, change in assignments will require an act of Congress," Mansfield said with a grin. I expect us to hit the ground running with a full agenda by the end of the month.

As we left the capital building, a younger man, perhaps in his forties, approached me, "Not a good move getting called out on your first day," he said. "I'm Mike Spinelli. I represent the tenth district in New Mexico. Four of us newbies are meeting at Bullfeathers to compare notes. Would you join us?"

Mike ushered me to a table in the back and introduced me to the others. There was Susan Dillingham, Arizona's third district; Robert (Bob) Mally, Kansas's first district; and Premoday Khakha, representing Utah's second district. "What am I, your token New England Yankee?" I said, sitting down.

"Yes," said Susan, "now order."

I got my hamburger and beer. We talked about our backgrounds and why we each ran for office, and in general had a pleasant couple of hours together.

Bob remembered seeing my name associated with the terrorist plot to poison New York City's water. This launched me into stories about Maxi. Susan was a dog lover and wanted to meet Mazi. "Maybe later, she's back in Boston with my wife," I said.

"Where are you staying?" Mike asked.

"I'm in a hotel right now, looking for a cheap place to stay. Carol, my wife, wants me to commute on weekends; she has no interest in leaving Boston."

"I'm leasing a basement apartment, a ten-minute walk from Capitol Hill. It has two bedrooms. Interested in subletting?" said Mike.

13

At ten a.m., Friday morning George Mansfield from New Jersey was voted in to be the next Speaker of the House. The Republicans nominated their man, Tim Clark from Florida. He received two hundred sixteen votes, two shy from winning.

6 Politics

"Mr. Mansfield, I'm Sam Goodwin. I represent the 7th District of Massachusetts. I'd like to talk to you about committee assignments."

"Mr. Goodwin, yes, I've read about you and your dog Maxi. Please call me George, we're all one large family here. And you're Sam, or do you prefer Samual?"

"Sam is fine. One of the issues I ran on was the abusive policies of the Department of Homeland Security. This was the main driver for me being elected. My assignment to the Homeland Security Committee would go a long way in helping me keep my election promises. My predecessor was on this committee, and I was hoping to take her place."

"Sam, as you know committee assignments are based on seniority. I have three senior members vying for that open seat. There is not much I can do."

"Will we be seeing Maxi on Capitol Hill?" George asked as he dismissively turned away.

My congressional office was in the bowels of the Rayburn Building. My assigned receptionist was Mrs. Wanda Monro; she claimed no lineage to the former president. She was a middle-aged African American, five foot two, and was as wide as she was tall. My first encounter with her still rings in my ears, "Mr. Goodwin, I've been on Capitol Hill long before you got here, and I'll be here long after you leave. I know how things get done, so if you leave me alone to do my job, we'll get along fine." That was fine with me; at least one of us knew what I was doing.

Returning to my cavern after my interaction with Mansfield, Wanda handed me a note; "Congressman Smyth asked that you call upon him. His receptionist is one of those uppity college gals, don't trust her!"

Intrigued, I made my way to his suite of offices on the fourth floor of the Longworth Building. Something I could aspire to in twenty years. A young lady, Betty, according to her nameplate, was sitting behind the receptionist's desk.

"Betty, Congressman Smyth asked that I stop by. I'm Sam Goodwin."

"Please have a seat; the congressman is on the phone and will be a few minutes. Would you care for coffee or a soda?"

"No thank you, I'll just enjoy the sunlight."

Ten minutes later the congressman emerged and invited me into his office. "Please call me Tom ... Sam, isn't it? I only have a few minutes so let me get to the point. I understand you want to get on the Homeland Security Committee. I can make that happen. This will be my last tour in this zoo; I've announced my retirement. Several vultures are already after my committee seat."

"I represent the people of southern Maine," he continued. "There will be a vote later this year for a new ship, a naval reconnaissance ship. Will it be built at the Bath Shipyard or Newport News? If you commit your vote to me for Bath Shipyard, I'll step aside and name you as my committee replacement."

"You are bargaining for my vote?"

"Politics, my boy, politics. Are you in or not?"

"I'm in. What about the Speaker of the House? I thought he controlled committee assignments."

"Dirt, my boy. I've worked with George for close to twenty years and he wouldn't dare risk me airing dirty laundry. He'll do as I say."

That evening I was boasting to my new friends about my success at getting a committee assignment of my choice.

"So, you sold your vote," said Mike.

"A vote I would have made anyway to keep jobs in New England," I snapped back.

"Sounds like rationalization to me," murmured Premoday.

7   A Whiff of Trouble

I took a long weekend over Presidents' Day, returning to Boston to touch base with my constituents. Let's be real, to be with Carol and Maxi.

"Still no interest in moving to Washington?" I asked Carol. I checked some housing options out ... they are expensive. The ones we can almost afford don't allow pets, and those where Maxi would be welcomed are well beyond our means. Going further out, out into the wilderness of Stafford or Louden counties, it's a half-day commute to get to Capitol Hill. Well, maybe not that long, but over an hour each way."

"No, Maxi and I will stay in Boston. You promised you'd serve only one term, and I'm holding you to that. Perhaps I can visit you this summer, give you time to hide your personal assistant. Wanda sounds lovely on the phone."

"Tell Fenk I will tackle her problem in the next few weeks. The Director of Homeland Security is scheduled to appear before our committee in March. I'll challenge him about DHS's repatriation plans for refugees. He's looking for more money."

The following morning, with Maxi in tow, I visited *The Coffee Shope,* the second home for the cops from the local precinct. It was the best place to get the latest police gossip. I found Lieutenant Dolan at his usual table.

"Well, look who we have here," he managed to say as he pushed a chair out for me as he rubbed Maxi's ears. "Have you been corrupted by Washington yet?"

"Only sold my vote three times, netting me an office with a view of the Capital Building and a perky young secretary, which, by the way, don't mention the latter to Carol."

"In all seriousness, It's a boring job in the midst of egomaniacs. I've met a few good people. I got on the Homeland Security Committee and will tackle the refugee issue next month. But that's boring stuff for you; what's new in Boston?"

"The cold weather has kept the two-legged animals inside. We've had a rash of unexpected deaths. No violence and they do not appear to be overdoses. Victims are mostly elderly and reported to be in reasonably good health by their doctors. We are investigating to find any common links."

"And *Salt 'n Pepper?*" I asked. "I haven't heard from Danny or Jimmy since I went to DC."

"They've been staying out of trouble since you left. I think their latest client is one of the Tech firms. Something about the theft of intellectual property. They've teamed up with the Goodwin & Proctor law firm. Not a relative of yours, are they?" said Dolan.

"The firm's founder, Elisia Proctor, was my tenth-second cousin, twice removed. It's been years since I've been invited to a corporate Christmas party."

It was a bright winter day with the temperature in the low forties. *Salt 'n Pepper's* office on Charles Street was only a few blocks away so Maxi and I decided to walk, leaving my car in the parking garage.

Slipping quietly up the stairs, I released Maxi, and almost immediately heard Rossie's squeal of delighted surprise. "Sam, what are you doing here? You're supposed to be in DC cutting our taxes."

19

"I came back just to see you, Rossie. How are you doing?"

"The Emmerson Theater just finished its annual production of The Christmas Carol. I played Fred's wife. My main line, 'tight as a drum.' It was a fun production."

"Is Danny or Jimmy in?"

"No, they are over at the Goodwin & Proctor law firm. Any relation to you?"

8 DHS

"It's time you dragged your sorry ass in," said Wanda. "You white boys out parting all night, disgraceful."

"I'll let you know that I was in bed by eleven after spending most of the evening preparing for today's committee meeting with DHS."

"That weasel of a Secretary will probably tell the committee about the wonderful work he's doing with the border. And your Mayor was on the news last night bitching about the new immigrants Texas is sending her," said Wanda.

"The hearing starts at ten. I'll be in Danial's office until then. We want to coordinate our questions." Congressman Roy Danials, California District 25, is the Committee Chairman. Given DHS's Secretary's past performances before his committee, he wanted our questions coordinated. One to get an honest answer and two, to undercut Republican questioning.

At ten a.m. sharp Committee Chairman Danials banged the Homeland Security Committee into order. He asked the Sargent-at-Arms to swear in the witnesses, the Secretary of DHS, Benjamin Whitehead; the Director of the Border Patrol, Joray Gonzalez; and the Head of the Texas Rangers, Patrick McDonald.

For the next ninety minutes, Whitehead and Gonzalez told the committee under oath that McDonald was imagining the influx of migrants crossing the border, while McDonald provided sworn affidavits from communities along the Rio Grande as to migrants swarming their property.

Being the junior committee member, my turn to question the witnesses did not come until late morning. "Mr. Goodwin, it's almost time to break. Can you make your questions brief, or would you prefer to wait until this afternoon?" Chairman Danials asked.

"I'll make it brief Chairman Danials."

"Secretary Whitehead, my questions are on a different topic: repatriation of refugees. I understand you have directed the forced repatriation of Hatin refugees."

"That's a lie," he snapped back.

"And the Syrian refugees.

"You are misinformed."

"What about the Iraqi refugees?" I asked.

"I have not asked for the repatriation of any refugees," said the furious Secretary.

"I yield the rest of my time," I said.

As the committee members filed out, I asked the Chairman if I could have five minutes of his time. Looking at his watch, he said, "Yes, be in my office in one hour."

I was there waiting when he and another congressman returned from lunch. "Sam, I almost forgot you'd be here. The braised lamb in the congressional dining hall was excellent; hope you got some. What can I do for you?"

"I believe you want Benjamin Whitehead's scalp. He lied to the committee this morning."

"And what else is new? Can you prove it!"

"Yes. He testified this morning, under oath, about the repatriation of refugees. Here is a letter, signed by him, dated three months ago, directing the repatriation of Iraqi refugees in Boston."

"This is good," he said. "I was wondering where you were going this morning with your questions. This will make a good opening this afternoon."

At two o'clock the Homeland Security Committee was reconvened. "Secretary Whitehead, why did you lie to my college this morning? It has been brought to my attention that you personally directed the repatriation of Iraqi refugees. This letter signed by you three months ago contradicts your earlier testimony."

"I never signed such a letter. Can I see what you have?"

After the Sargent-at-Arms gave Whitehead the letter, and he made a show of studying it, the Secretary looked up and said, "That signature is a forgery."

"The signature looks very much like your other signatures," said Danials. I would like my document experts to take a look at it."

"Chairman, if I may, can I ask the witness one or two more questions?" I asked.

"Yes, but please make them brief."

"Secretary Whitehead, if that is not your signature, there is no repatriation order in effect for the Iraqi refugees in Boston. Is that correct?"

"Yes. That is what I testified to this morning."

The order to relocate the refugees to temporary housing on military facilities is null and void.

"Yes, that order never existed."

Thank you, no more questions.

23

Later that afternoon I called the Director of the Boston Iraqi Refugee Center and told him the DHS order relocating his people was sworn to be invalid by the Secretary of DHS. The Director should have his legal staff get a copy of today's Congressional Homeland Security Committee meeting and challenge, in court, the relocation proceedings that were already underway.

9 The Intrepid Five

Saturday morning, the intrepid five as we called ourselves: Mike Spinelli, Susan Dillingham, Bob Mally, Premoday Khakha, and myself - met for our weekly brunch and to compare notes on the previous week. We were all new to Congress, still feeling our way along.

Mike congratulated me on my questioning of Benjamin Whitchead. "He's a slippery dog that needed to be knocked down a notch or two. That bastard has flooded the southwest with illegals. When challenged, he sits back and smirks."

"How did you get on the Homeland Security Committee?" asked Susan. "That's a plumb committee assignment."

"A fellow sympathetic New England politician made it possible," I said. "But enough about me, what's going on in your lives."

"My constituents have noted an increase in elderly deaths," said Bob. "The State's Center for Disease Control agrees the number of deaths is outside statistical norms but has not identified the cause."

"Susan, how did you get an office with a window?" I asked. I'm stuck in the bowels of the Rayburn Building. My one bright spot is my receptionist, Wanda. She's more in tune with the House than most senior members.

"I'll trade my office for Wanda. My receptionist is a newly graduated college airhead," said Susan. "All she is concerned about is her date for the weekend. Maybe I'll send her your way Premoday; she'd liven your life up."

"Is that before or after my wife takes a pound of my flesh."

Speaking of wives, Sam, you said your wife would be bringing your dog to DC for a visit. When's that going to happen? All you talk about is Maxi – that's not a very flattering name for a significant other," said Susan.

***

Monday morning I'm in the office early only to be greeted by Wanda wanting to know why I'm keeping banker hours.

"Sam, you had a call from a Maggie O'Brien. She said you knew her. From the sound of her voice, I don't think I'd cross her if I were you."

"That would be Mayor O'Brien, the mayor of Boston, and your perception is correct; there are many bodies on the wayside that have tried to cross her."

"Mayor O'Brien, this is Congressman Goodwin returning your call."

"Congressman is it. You're my favorite dog handler and Maxi is 'the dog.'" she said jokingly. "I saw your performance on the public network last week; brilliant. But that is not why I'm calling. There has been a recent uptick in elderly deaths. My public health department thinks they have it narrowed down to an over-the-counter health supplement that's widely advertised. They've contacted the Food and Drug Administration but received a bland response. I'm calling to see if you have time to follow-up."

"Interesting. A fellow freshman congressman mentioned an unusual number of elderly deaths in New Mexico. I'll look into it."

After I hung the phone up, I drafted an email to the intrepid five.

Saturday Bob mentioned an unusual increase in elderly deaths in New Mexico. This morning I received a phone call from the mayor of Boston with the same observation. Her people think they've narrowed the cause of these deaths down to an over-the-counter health supplement that's widely advertised. My question is, have you received similar complaints from your constituents?

By noon the next day, I received replies that Utah and Arizona were also recording an increase in the elderly death rate. My follow-up response was, "Okay, what do we do now?"

As an office practice, I cc'd Wanda on all my email correspondence. Minutes later, after hitting the send key, Wanda was in my office asking who I knew on the Subcommittee on Health Care and Financial Services.

"No one as far as I know," I said. "Who does this subcommittee report to?"

"The Committee on Oversight and Accountability. You need to get one of your buddies on that committee," said Wanda.

"And I just wander into Mansfield's office asking to place so-n-so on that committee."

"It's not a sought-after committee assignment," said Wanda. "If one of your group is not already on it, I can get Mansfield's secretary to make it happen."

10 FDA

As it turned out Mike Spinelli had been assigned to the Committee on Oversight and Accountability. It was a committee he had no interest in, but being a dutiful freshman house member, he attended the committee's hearings. The growing number of elderly deaths in New Mexico prompted his interest in the FDA, 'what was causing these deaths.'

Meanwhile, back home, Mayor O'Brien directed the city's health department to look into the growing number of deaths in Boston and statewide.

Two weeks later the Mayor called to give me an update. "Sam, our preliminary findings found probable links to a homeopathic health supplement sold under two brands. *Gerontological Renovation* and *Gerontologisk Løft*. Both claim to help mental acuity in the geriatric set, although most customers don't recall which band they've been taking.

"Wei Sing, LLC, a provider of traditional Chinese medicine, markets Gerontological Renovation. Wei Sing imports all its products from Taiwan.

"Gerontologisk Løft is produced locally by NorthernLights Holistic Alternatives, Inc., in New Hampshire. The firm is under license from Hansen AG, a Norwegian holistic drug marketer.

"At this time, we don't know if one or both, or neither are the cause of these deaths. My health department will continue to investigate. I've directed the health department to engage *Salt 'n Pepper* to assist in the investigation."

At our next Saturday brunch, I conveyed Mayor O'Brien's information, omitting the part about *Salt 'n Pepper*.

"I've made some progress," said Mike. "I've got myself assigned to the Subcommittee on Health Care and Financial Services. Can you believe there is no interest in being on that subcommittee? I thought the Oversight and Accountability Chairwoman was going to kiss me when I volunteered."

"When will you be able to question the FDA Director," asked Susan.

"It's Commissioner," said Mike, "and she's scheduled to meet with the subcommittee next week. Martha Madison will be defending the FDA's budget request. I sent her an email with information about these deaths and asked that she be prepared to discuss the issue."

***

"Commissioner Madison, thank you for getting back to me on my question regarding an uptick in elderly deaths in the several States I identified," said Mike **Spinelli**. "Based on preliminary findings by the Boston Health Department and confirmed by several other departments across the country. Two homeopathic health supplements, Gerontological Renovation and Gerontologisk Løft, may be linked to these deaths. Have your people had a chance to look into this?"

"Congressman Spinelli, thank you for your interest in this. Reviewing raw monthly data the FDA collects, there does appear to be a statistical increase in senior deaths. As for the products

Gerontological Renovation and Gerontologisk Løft, I have opened a file to look into them."

"As you know," continued Commissioner Madison, "there are minimal regulations on holistic products after they pass our initial review. They are sold over-the-counter in a buyer-beware market. We only get involved when there are outlandish claims or when there is a health threat ... as you claim here. Their marketing claim is that they enhance mental alertness, which has neither been confirmed nor proven false. I have no other information on them at this time. I will get back to you when we know more."

Later that afternoon Susan is saying to us, "Typical bureaucratic stonewalling. What can we do?"

"Leak it to the press?" suggested Premoday.

"No, I don't think we have enough to work with," I said. "We could be sued for slander."

"Boston's health department is investigating the deaths. Can you pull strings in your States and suggest they work with Massachusetts? We need to find a medical link."

11 Brunch

Carol came for a visit shortly after the congressional summer recess. The visit was timed with a book signing in Old Town Alexandria for her latest novel, <u>The Gentleman</u>. It was about an international spy, one with no loyalties, selling State secrets. It wasn't just another spy novel; it was about an old man, once a fearless spy in bygone decades, now just a shell of himself trying to regain relevancy in a world of new technology. <u>The Gentleman</u> was now number three on the New York best sellers list.

Since the book signing was being held in Old Town's Barnes & Noble, the intrepid five decided to hold our Saturday morning brunch in the courtyard of the *Alexandrian* in Old Town, where Carol was staying. The hotel made special accommodations for Maxi and even allowed me to spend the weekend.

Carol and I were just seated when my four colleagues arrived. Introductions were made, and coffee ordered. Maxi sat at my side, between Carol and myself. As the brunch proceeded, I caught Carol slipping Maxi a strip of bacon – just after the piece I gave her. "Carol, we can't keep feeding her from the table; she'll lose her girlish trim."

"She looks a bit over the hill to me," said Mike. "What, is she thirteen or fourteen years old? Let her enjoy life."

Fortunately, we were at a table off to the side of the courtyard. "Did you say over the hill?" Looking at Mike, I pointed and commanded, "MAXI WATCH." The dog was on her feet and just behind Mike's chair before he could respond. As he started to get up, Maxi emitted a growl that would send shivers down the spine of most dog handlers.

After a bit more chit-chat about politics, Carol's book, and Mike's predicament, we got up to leave; Mike was left at the table, prevented from moving without the threat of bodily harm from Maxi.

At Carol's insistence, I returned to the table and ordered Maxi to stand down. As Mike got up, I took his hand and said, "Maxi, Friend." Maxi came up to him, sniffed his crotch, and sat down, wagging her tail.

"Okay Mike, you are now a member of Maxi's inner circle."

***

As I said, the book signing was at the local Barnes & Noble, scheduled for one to three that afternoon. Since Maxi was, or her alias Sheila, a featured player in The Gentleman, the store provided a dog bed next to Carol's table, on the left side, for Maxi. Most of Carol's fans approached the opposite side of the table, but a few ventured closer to Maxi, earning a tail wag.

Although the book signing was scheduled to end at three, there were still a few fans in line waiting to get a signed copy. Carol agreed to give it another fifteen minutes. Now, if we had just left at the scheduled time, we could have missed the chaos.

There were gunshots outside the store followed by police sirens from multiple squad cars. Three hooded men 'fell' through the front door. One obviously shot in the leg. The tallest of the three, apparently the leader, ordered all the customers onto the floor while grabbing one of the salesclerks to use as a shield. Carol and I were in

32

the back of the store behind a couple of shelves of books. "Stay out of this Sam," she whispered, "the police will handle it."

Looking at her, I whispered back, "The police can always use a little help," as Maxi and I started to slip down the aisle between the shelves.

Nearing the front of the store, I found myself separated from two of the gunmen by one rack of books and the third, holding the hostage, no more than twenty feet to their left. The rack was temporary, placed there to hold a promotional display. As I toppled the book rack, I released Maxi on the hostage holder. Jumping over the mass of books covering the two punks, I kicked the first in the head and grabbed his gun. The second, the one with the leg wound, was bleeding out and was not a threat. I called Maxi off and ordered the third punk, now with a bleeding arm, to the ground.

I told one of the sales clerks to open the door for the police but first to call out to tell them what she was doing. I didn't want any young rookie getting trigger-happy. As the police entered, I was ordered to drop the gun and put my hands on my head. They didn't know what to do with Maxi, who by then was standing at my side.

Once a police sergeant was on site, it took only a few minutes for me to confirm my identity and start getting high-fives from the three officers who were now cuffing the two punks and applying a tourniquet to the third.

The following Monday Wanda looked up as I entered my cave and said, "Couldn't stay out of the news could you?" as she held up Sunday's Washington Post with a highlighted article.

Massachusetts Congressman Sam Goodwin captures three gunmen police were chasing after a failed armed bank robbery in Alexandria Saturday afternoon. He was assisted by his dog Maxi. The congressman is a retired Boston police canine handler. Maxi, a large German Shepherd, retired with him. They were at the Alexandria Old Town Barnes & Noble *promoting Carol Goodman's latest novel, <u>The Gentleman,</u> which is on the NYT bestseller list when the gunmen burst into the store attempting to evade the police.*

12   A Lead

"Danny O'Kaye is on the line. Do you want to talk to him?" asked Wanda.

Picking the receiver up I said to Wanda so he could hear me, "I shouldn't waste my time; he's always blowing smoke."

"Hi Danny, what's new in Boston?"

"Blowing smoke! I'll show you smoke next time you come home."

"The Boston Globe had a snippet the other day about our congressman playing hero."

"Maxi needed a little exercise, but what are you calling for? I'm sure it wasn't just to break my chops."

"No, you're right. Mayor O'Brien, or more accurately, the Mayor's health department, contracted with Jimmy and me two months ago to see what we could find out about the two holistic over-the-counter tablets Gerontological Renovation and Gerontologisk Løft."

"Yes, I know she told me. Have you found anything of interest?"

"Gerontological Renovation is marketed by Wei Sing, LLC, a provider of traditional Chinese medicine. Wei Sing is a small provider of traditional holistic medicines. They appear to be an above-board company. Over two decades selling their products in the States with no complaints.

"Now, on the other hand, Gerontologisk Løft is produced locally by NorthernLights Holistic Alternatives, Inc. NorthernLights is a subsidiary of ACME-Pharma, Inc. You may recall that ACME-Pharma was the center of a drug contamination lawsuit a decade ago. They pleaded no contest and were fined over a hundred million dollars.

"Gerontologisk Løft is produced under license from Hansen AG, a Norwegian holistic drug marketer. Jimmy, working undercover at their plant in New Hampshire, found that the main ingredient for Gerontologisk Løft, polymoxlymeth, is imported, shipments coming through the port of Boston. Now guess where those shipments originate. If you say Norway, you'd be wrong. They come from Guizhou Province in China.

"Now being the cynic that I am, I did a little research. The cost of this ingredient in China is about one-third of its cost in Norway."

"You guys might be on to something," I said. Two questions: Who have you told, and has this ingredient been tested in a lab?"

"We gave the Mayor our findings last week, and she tasked the health department to analyze it. Due to staffing shortages in the lab, we don't expect results until the end of the month, another ten days."

"Thanks for the update Danny; I'll give Maxi your love," I said with a chuckle as I disconnected.

Later that week I gave the other members of the Intrepid Five an update. I suggested to Mike he might pass the information on to his FDA contact.

When we first became aware of an uptick in elderly deaths among our constituents, we started asking other House members if they noted a similar trend. Several did. In the past several weeks other House members reported similar trends.

When it appeared possible that these deaths may have been caused by an over-the-counter drug, Mike questioned the FDA Commissioner. Although the FDA acknowledged the increase in geriatric deaths (the term they used), they exhibited little interest in pursuing the issue, focusing instead on mask mandates in anticipation of a COVID reoccurrence.

Early the following month I found Wanda on the phone with Danny, "That can't be true," she was saying, "he'd never do anything like that, would he?" Seeing me, she reverted to her office voice and said Mr. O'Kaye is on line two."

"What lies are you spreading now Danny?" I said as I picked up the receiver.

"We got the lab results back yesterday. There were traces of mushrooms in our samples," said Danny. "Traces of mushrooms similar to magic mushrooms. Apparently, the equipment used to process the ingredients for Gerontologisk Løft is also used to process mushrooms used in traditional Chinese medicine.

"They also found chemical impurities commonly found in commercial-grade polymoxlymeth. These impurities can be deadly.

"The health department thinks a microscopic trace could cause death in a senior having certain health problems. They have contacted the Harvard Medical School for further study of both the mushrooms and polymoxlymeth impurities."

"That's good Danny. Thanks for the information. I'll pass it on to my group for action. Tell Mayor O'Brien to keep pressing from her end."

13   Inaction

"Sending the elderly on a magical trip," joked Bob Mally.

"That is most insensitive," said Susan.

"Explains why the Gen Z crowd are buying the stuff," said Premoday.

We were at our Saturday brunch the day after Danny's call, and I had just relayed what Danny had told me.

"Mike, does the Oversight and Accountability Committee have any upcoming hearings? Perhaps one focused on the FDA where you can question Commissioner Madison."

"Just by chance we do. The FDA is looking to finalize next year's budget this coming week."

***

"Commissioner Madison, last time we had a chance to talk I asked about a spike in senior deaths. About the possible connection with two over-the-counter health products. Since then, I've done a bit more research and narrowed the problem to Gerontologisk Løft. I found that its main ingredient, polymoxlymeth, is manufactured in Guizhou Province in China. Medical opinion suggests it is a tossup as to which is killing our seniors: magic mushrooms or impurities in polymoxlymeth," Mike said as he started his turn of questions.

"I am unaware of this," said Madison. "Perhaps you can share your sources with us."

"The Boston Public Health Department has, which I believe was in contact with your people," Mike fired back.

If that's the case, it has not reached my desk. Let me get back to you," she said with little conviction.

14 Washington Post

"Mr. Congressman, there is a reporter from the Washington Post on hold wanting to talk to you about an interview," said Wanda. "Don't let this go to your head. These bottom feeders will interview anyone who's breathing, and if not breathing, they'll make the interview up."

Picking the receiver up, "Good morning, this is Sam Goodwin. I understand you're a reporter with the Washington Post."

"Thank you for taking my call congressman. I'm Ron Abdow. Yes, I'm with the Washington Post and write the Capital Hill Column, where I discuss items of public interest and introduce new congressional members to my readers. I would like to do a sit-down interview with you if you are available. You're new to Congress, have an interesting background, and made quite a splash in last Sunday's paper. Our readers would like to get to know you better."

"I have a rather busy schedule this week. I can squeeze you in after three this Thursday."

"Excellent," said Abdow, "I look forward to talking with you."

Thursday came around faster than I expected. I'd forgotten about my promised interview when Wanda was standing at my door and said, "The bottom feeder is here."

As the reporter entered my office, he said, "She doesn't have much regard for reporters does she."

"Don't mind Wanda, she's like that with everyone. Okay, you're here to interview me. What do you want to know?"

"Congressman Goodwin, everything, but my first question is, what got you into politics?"

"First, please call me Sam. This congressman thing is still new to me. But to your question, my neighbor is an Iraqi refugee. There were fears in the refugee community that they would be forcibly repatriated. I went to Mayor O'Brien, mayor of Boston, seeking help for my neighbor. The Mayor told me she had no leverage and if I wanted to do something, I should run for Congress. The DNC was looking for a candidate for the 7th District. I unexpectedly won the race."

I then went on to talk about seeking a committee assignment where I could question Benjamin Whitehead, Secretary of DHS.

"Sam, the Homeland Security Committee is one of the more sought-after committee assignments. How did you end up on it?"

"Congressman Smyth from Maine is retiring after this term. He has been on this committee for many years and wanted his seat taken by a like-minded Yankee. He convinced Speaker Mansfield to make the assignment."

"That's rather unusual, isn't it?" asked Ron.

"Smyth and Mansfield have a history going back a couple of decades; you'd have to ask them. It could be nothing more than Mansfield calling in an old 'marker' before he retired."

"Going back into your past, I see you retired from the Boston Police Department where you were a dog handler. You and your partner, Maxi I think it is, received several citations. In retirement, you joined the *Salt 'n Pepper Detective Agency*. Can you elaborate on any of this?"

41

I spent the next twenty minutes reliving my recent experiences working with Danny and Jimmy.

"Sounds like you've been more active since you retired than you were in the BPD," said Ron.

"That's what my wife keeps telling me," I said.

"Okay, almost done here," said the reporter. Your roommate, Mike Spinelli, has been aggressively questioning FDA Commissioner Martha Madison about deaths caused by the holistic medicine Gerontologisk Løft. I understand you are the driving force behind Spinelli in this quest."

"I am one of several House members concerned about the uptick in elderly deaths, deaths we believe are caused by Gerontologisk Løft."

"This sounds to be a noble cause, congressman, but could this be a problem in that ACME-Pharma is a major contributor to the DNC? Gerontologisk Løft is produced by NorthernLights Holistic Alternatives, a subsidiary of ACME-Pharma."

***

That Sunday's edition of the Washington Post carried Ron's Capitol Hill Column."

> *Congressman Sam Goodwin (D-MA) appears to be the force behind recent attacks by Congressman Mike Spinelli (D-NM) on the Food and Drug Administration. The claim that mounting senior deaths can be attributed to Gerontologisk Løft, a holistic medicine produced by one of ACME-Pharma's subsidiaries, can be traced back to Congressman Goodwin. ACME-Pharma is one of the DNC's major contributors.*

15 Fallout

'That bottom feeder scum,' I was muttering to myself. "You were right, Wanda; they are nothing but bottom feeders,' I said as I arrived at my windowless office Monday morning.

"Can't stay out of the news can you? You have several phone messages requesting a callback. But this one you should take; Speaker Mansfield wants you in his office now. His secretary suggested it was urgent."

I spent the next half hour cooling my heels in Mansfield's outer office. The secretary not offering coffee was an indication of the deep doo-doo I was in.

When finally admitted to the inner sanctum, I found the House Speaker and the House Majority Whip, Congressman Richards from New York. "What the hell is this!" shouted Mansfield, holding up the Washington Post's Health Section. Are you trying to alienate one of our major campaign donors?"

"I was sandbagged."

"That's no excuse; that's why we have a public affairs office. Weren't you told that all interviews should be coordinated by them?"

"I've had three calls from ACME-Pharma's public affairs office this morning wanting to know how we'll fix this."

"Fix what?" I asked. "The deaths are real, Harvard Medical School concurs that Gerontologisk Løft is the probable cause, and FDA is dithering."

"Midterm elections are coming up. This inquiry into ACME-Pharma will impact donations. Get Spinelli to back off until after the elections."

"And ignore the needs of my constituents? No, Spinelli can make his own decisions," I righteously said as I started to get up to leave.

"Don't you dare get uppity!" said Richards. "If you can't support the Party's program, you might find yourself isolated."

Later that day I got an unexpected visit from Congressman Smyth.

"Nice office; I haven't been this deep underground in years," said my visitor. I see Wanda is your receptionist. She's been here since my first year in Congress. Over the years, several of 'her' freshman politicians have tried to enticer her to move upstairs with her. Her response, 'They're easier to intimidate down here.' I think the truth is she feels a calling to help freshman members navigate the politics of the House. Anyway, you're damn lucky to have her."

"Now, about this misunderstanding you're having with the Speaker, any chance of backing down?"

"No."

"Didn't think so. Just so you know, I'm in your court. A close family friend recently died. Doctors attribute his death to a homeopathic medicine. George's cognitive abilities were slipping and the ads for Gerontologisk Løft promised improved mental alertness. I take it this is the same story your group is getting from their constituents."

"Almost line for line. Mayor O'Brien first brought these deaths to my attention. The Harvard Medical School made its findings public, and my former colleagues found the smoking gun pointing back to

NorthernLights. I think you recall that ACME-Pharma was the center of a drug contamination lawsuit a decade ago. They are at it again."

"And they are one of the DNC's major donors," said Tom. "Several congressional members owe their seats to ACME's deep pockets."

"The Speaker will move to remove you from the Homeland Security Committee. When he does, remind him of his promise to me and mention the name Mildred," said Tom.

"Mildred?"

"Dirty laundry that's best left buried," said Congressman Smyth.

***

Three days later Mansfield summoned me to his office. There were no others present. He informed me I was being removed from the Homeland Security Committee.

"If I'm permitted to ask, why?" I asked.

"Since we last talked, I had a friendly chat with Congressman Spinelli. He agreed that without hard scientific evidence, he would lay off ACME-Pharma. He'll have no more embarrassing questions for Commissioner Madison. As for your question, why ... we need people on that committee that support the Party line."

"My advocate, Congressman Smyth, predicted you would have me removed, reneging on your promise to him. He suggested I remind you of 'Mildred,' whoever that is."

"The Speaker, turning bright red, started sputtering, ordering me out of his office."

45

16 Malcontents

That night after meeting with Mansfield, I confronted Mike with Mansfield's comments.

"Is it true you'll drop questioning Commissioner Madison about ACME-Pharma?"

Looking embarrassed, he confirmed Mansfield's statement. "Sam, listen, proof of Gerontologisk Løft's detrimental effects has not been proven. Our current information will not stand a legal challenge."

"Come off it Mike, you were bought. Findings by Harvard Medical School carry weight: ingredient adulteration is criminal, and the pattern of deaths is convincing. What did you get?"

"I can stay on the subcommittee and perhaps do some good in the future. I also have an uphill challenge for reelection. Mansfield promised funding for my political action committee."

In my nightly call to Carol, well, almost nightly, I told her of the day's events. My removal from the committee was a disappointment, but Tom's sellout was unsettling. "I'm thinking of looking for new lodgings," I said. "I'm not sure I can trust him in the future."

"Don't do anything rash. Think about it for a couple of days. When I met Mike, he seemed trustworthy. Perhaps he had reasons you don't know about," Carol advised. "And if I can ask, who is Mildred?"

***

Two days later a short article by Ron Abdow appeared in the Washington Post.

> *Solyndra revisited. Readers may remember the demise of Solyndra fifteen years ago. Solyndra, a recipient of a half-billion-dollar federal subsidy, and the company's subsequent bankruptcy. The company's CFO was Mildred Gaston. She was the only company officer charged with defrauding the US Government, was found guilty, and is now serving a twenty-year sentence. At a recent parole hearing, the House Speaker, George Mansfield, appeared on her behalf. Congressman Mansfield was a strong supporter of the subsidy to Solyndra. Unsubstantiated rumors at the time suggested he and Mildred were having an affair.*

***

That Saturday the intrepid five met for brunch as usual. Mike was the last to arrive giving us time to discuss his apparent betrayal of our interests ... protection of our elderly constituents. It was an uncomfortable brunch. We wanted to attack him but didn't. He wanted to defend his actions but didn't.

I mentioned Mansfield had removed me from the Homeland Security Committee because of my stance on ACME-Pharma. I received words of support from Susan, Bab, and Premoday. Mike was unusually quiet, not his usual bombastic self.

Susan's district had one of the highest senior death rates, notable even in Arizona with all its retirement communities. "Mike, enough with all this pussy footing around, what did you do? What deal did you cut?" she asked.

"What are you talking about? I didn't make any deals."

"Why have you backed off questioning Commissioner Madison?"

"You have no right to judge my actions on the subcommittee; what has Sam been telling you?" he said while looking at me.

47

Mike then got up, threw some money on the table, then stalked out of the restaurant.

Premoday noted, "I guess we're now the intrepid four."

"Well, I guess I should start looking for a new place to stay. I'm subletting from Mike."

"My condo in Fairlington Village has a few vacant studio apartments. You could carpool with Premoday and me," said Bob.

"Where is Fairlington Village?" I asked.

"It's an older neighborhood in Arlington. It definitely doesn't have the access to Capitol Hill of your current digs, but the neighbors are more trustworthy. After we finish here, Premoday and I will take you over to see what they can do for you."

Later that day I told Mike I planned to move out by the end of the week.

"Not a problem here," he said. "I was going to ask you to leave by the end of the month. I recently promised your room to an old college buddy."

17 Trouble

After Abdow's article revisiting Solyndra, Mansfield was under pressure to step down from the speakership by the newer House members. Most of the 'old guard' remained in his camp providing sufficient numbers for him to hold his position.

In addition to **Ron's Capitol Hill Column,** Ron manages an online blog 'Capitol Hill Gossip.' Early the following month he posted his critique of the House.

A small band of House members, led by Congressman Sam Goodwin, continues to seek justice for seniors whose golden years were cut short by an adulterated holistic medicine, specifically Gerontologisk Løft. *This writer understands that the Boston Department of Public Health has documented the import of suspected ingredients. NorthernLights Holistic Alternatives, Inc., the producer of Gerontologisk Løft, is under license from Hansen AG, a Norwegian holistic drug marketer. It is this writer's understanding that Hansen AG is in the process of terminating said license for unspecified reasons. Congressman Goodwin was rewarded for seeking the truth by Speaker Mansfield ... by being removed from the prestigious Homeland Security Committee. Why? NorthernLights is a subsidiary of ACME-Pharma, a major donor to many incumbents. Readers may remember that ACME-Pharma was the center of a drug contamination lawsuit a decade ago. This writer wonders if they are up to their old tricks.*

Returning to my office after Abdow's latest posting had time to make its rounds on Capitol Hill, Wanda confronted me, "I've just about got you trained; now you are the pariah within your Party. I've had three meeting cancellations in the last hour." Just as Wanda was getting into stride, **Congressman Smyth** walked in.

"Sam, I haven't seen so much gnashing of teeth since Clinton's 'zipper-gate' scandal. Don't get discouraged; let's see where this goes. I'm in your corner," said Tom.

"And this from a lame-duck legislator who has announced his retirement," I said, thanking him.

Abdow's blog went viral on the internet. Constituents across the country were pestering their elected members of Congress as to what they were doing. Many cited the loss of loved ones.

18 Home Invasion

Sunday morning I received an urgent call from Danny. "There was a break-in at your home last night; Carol is in the hospital. Maxi nearly killed one of the intruders and crippled the second. The police have both in custody. Carol was not seriously hurt. Lieutenant Doyle thought it would be best if the doctors checked her out. One of the intruders gave her a good smack on the head."

"I'll be on the next plane."

Later that afternoon Danny and Lieutenant Doyle met me at Logan Airport, and with a police escort, we headed to the hospital.

"Carol, are you okay?" I cried out as I entered the hospital room.

She was sitting up in bed working on her laptop. "I understand I'm doing better than my two visitors."

I turned to Doyle, "What happened?"

"About eleven thirty last night 911 received a call from your neighbor, Fenk, reporting a disturbance at your home. A patrol car was dispatched. The officer, a young man new to the BPD, found the front door open and went in. Carol was holding a small pillow to a man's neck trying to stanch the flow of blood. He immediately called for an ambulance. The tech later treated Carol for what appeared to be a serious blow to the head. That's why she's here.

51

"Carol said in her statement that the two intruders broke in as she was tidying up, getting ready for bed. Maxi was on the first one, taking a chunk of meat from his leg when the second guy hit her in the head with his pistol. Maxi went nuts, lighting into him. By the time Carol could get Maxi off, his windpipe was crushed, and his carotid artery punctured. She was applying pressure to stop the blood flow when the officer arrived. The officer's partner followed the blood trail from the house and found the second attacker collapsed on the sidewalk from loss of blood."

"Why?" I asked. "Did you question them?"

"Not yet. One is obviously not going to be talking for a while, if ever. His larynx was crushed. The second is still unconscious."

"I want to be there when you question him."

"Now you know I can't do that."

"Then I'll call in the federal marshals. This was an attack on the family of a congressional member," I said.

Looking at me, Doyle said, "I see you are serious. Okay, be here at one tomorrow. Since he can't come downtown, we plan to integrate him here."

***

At twelve-thirty the next day I was escorted to the hospital's small but secure wing, reserved for police detainees requiring medical attention. Doyle was waiting for me. Handing me a paper cup of coffee, he said, "Let's establish some rules. You stand in the back and be quiet. If you have a question, let me know and I'll ask it. Understood?"

We entered the hospital room. Earl Wilson was handcuffed to the bed. Earl had a long rap sheet of mostly small strong-arm crimes and assaults. He was one of the City's underground enforces working for Pauli Palson who ran several backroom poker games, among other questionable activities.

"Good morning, Earl," started Doyle; "get a good night's sleep? That dog did a job on your leg."

"That dog needs to be put down," snapped Earl.

"Now, what were you doing attacking that lady last night?"

"We had the wrong house; it was supposed to be a surprise birthday party."

Well, the dog differs with you; says you broke in and started assaulting her mistress."

"Screw the dog!" snapped Earl.

Doyle turned to me and said, "Sam, you wait here. I need to talk with the guard in the hall. I'll be back in five minutes. And please don't disturb Mr. Wilson."

As Doyle closed the door, I moved over to Earl's bed and not so gently grabbed his injured leg. Squeezing his thigh, I said, "Earl, let's talk."

As his screaming subsided, he exclaimed, "That's police brutality!"

"I'm not with the police. I'm the husband. The dog you want to put down is Maxi, my dog." With another squeeze, I asked, "Why?"

After a repeat of whys and squeezes, Earl finally gasped, "Pauli sent us."

When Doyle reentered the room, he looked at Earl and observed, "Your dressing is leaking blood. I'll get the nurse to look in on you when we leave. Now, what do you mean Pauli sent you?"

In the next few minutes, Earl told us his story. Pauli had sent them to rough up the lady and leave a message, "Tell your husband to stand down."

"Why," asked Doyle. "What is Paulie's interest?"

"I don't know," grimaced Earl. "Get the nurse. ... Pauli sent us after he was visited by some business types, men in fancy suits. Please, my leg is killing me."

As we left the hospital, Doyle told me about that day's morning meeting with the Mayor as relayed by Chief Daniels.

As told by the Chief, he was reporting about the assault on Carol; the City's Director for Animal Control jumped in to say a vicious dog like that needed to be quarantined. The Mayor, in a voice that would freeze an ice cube, looked at him, 'Ralph, if I hear that again from you or anyone in animal control, you'll be fired on the spot.'

"The Mayor has Maxie's back," said Doyle.

19 Pauli's Choice

We arrived at Pauli Palson's office in North Boston accompanied by three cruisers and a squad of police. Entering the premises in a style reminiscent of Eliot Ness, Doyle slapped his search warrant down on Pauli's desk.

"Pauli talk to us," he demanded.

Totally befuddled and with a moment's hesitation "about what?"

Doyle looked around and directed the sergeant to start his search with the filing cabinets.

"Tell me about Earl and his buddy."

It was obvious that word of their failed midnight assault had failed or that the two were in police custody.

"What about them? I haven't seen Earl recently."

"Don't lie to me Pauli," said Doyle. "You ordered Earl and his buddy to attack Mrs. Goodwin at her home. Earl is in the hospital, talking, and his buddy is on life support."

Pauli, somewhat taken aback, stammered, "What are you talking about?"

"Well, Mr. Palson, my men are going to start taking this place apart until your memory improves," said Doyle.

"Stop! Let's talk," squealed Pauli. Last week two men came here wanting to hire my men to deliver a message. I told them I wasn't in the messenger business, but Earl might be interested if the price was right. I didn't send them; they were freelancing."

"Who were these men," I asked.

Snapping his head around to me, Pauli snaps, "Who's he?"

"Just an interested party, but I suggest you answer him," responded Doyle.

Looking down at his feet, Pauli said they claimed to be with NorthernLights.

"And why would they come to you," asked Doyle.

"I've done some work for their CEO, Carl Kitchener, in the past."

"What kind of work?"

"I'll take the 5th on that," mumbled Pauli.

20   The Feds

Driving back to headquarters, Doyle made an abrupt turn and headed toward Chelsea.

"Where are we going? Your office is in the other direction."

"NorthernLights is located in New Hampshire, outside my jurisdiction. We need to talk with Agent Bixby," he replied.

Agent Bixby was one of the senior agents in the FBI's Boston field office. We worked with her last year when Salt 'n Pepper tracked IRA terrorists and the year earlier, the Islamic jihadists. She was on Maxi's list of approved people.

Arriving at the federal building, Lieutenant Doyle identified himself and had the guard call Agent Bixby. After a few brief words, she turned to Doyle, "Seventh floor, elevators on the left."

Joyce was waiting for us when the elevator doors opened. "I'm intrigued; how can the lowly FBI help Boston's finest today? And Congressman Goodwin, I'm honored."

"It's a long story. Can we use one of your conference rooms?" said Doyle.

He started with the uptick in local elderly deaths. "The suspension was that these deaths were caused by the holistic medicine Gerontologisk Løft. Our investigation indicated that the imported ingredient, polymoxlymeth, was industrial-grade and not meant for human consumption. Concurrent with the City of Boston's efforts, Sam, in his legislator role, initiated efforts in Congress to look into the production of Gerontologisk Løft. It turns out several States were reporting an increased death rate in seniors. NorthLights is a subsidiary of ACME-Pharma, a major political donor. Sam was 'directed' by the Speaker of the House to stop pushing. Well, you know Sam, he kept digging. As a warning, Carol was attacked late Friday night at home. She's in the hospital, nothing serious but the two attackers, one on life support, are also there. They didn't count on Maxi."

"My god," said Joyce, "an attack on a sitting member of Congress's family to influence legislation is a federal offense. Has this been reported to federal marshals? What have you done?"

"No, you're the federal cops. I think it's in your court. As for what we've done…"

Agent Bixby called the field office's Director and reported what she had just been told. He cleared his calendar and had the three of us in his office on the eighth floor, where Lieutenant Doyle and I repeated the story.

"I agree with the Lieutenant," said the Director. "It's our case; the marshals will only muck it up. Agent Bixby, Joyce, you have the lead on this. I want daily reports. I'll coordinate with the Capital Hill police; they have jurisdiction since they are responsible for the safety of legislators."

Leaving the federal building the three of us returned to the hospital where I left them and went to Carol's room; she was being discharged. Doyle and Bixby went to Earl's room to get a 'federal' confession since the assault had moved into the federal legal arena.

I found Carol dressed and ready to go. "I've been waiting for you; where have you been?"

I filled her in on my day, saying Doyle and I made some headway, and the FBI was now working on the case.

"Where is Maxi?" she asked.

Doyle said Danny had her. I'll go and get her as soon as I get you home.

21 FBI-Boston

Agent Bixby had just given Earl the good news: his crimes would be tried in federal court. Assault on a congressman or on his family to sway his vote was worth a twenty year sentence. Earl was cursing Pauli when Bixby and Doyle left his room.

"I've asked my people to bring Mr. Palson in for questioning. Would you like to join me?" said Joyce.

It was early evening, but Doyle had nothing better to do. "Let's do it," he answered.

When the two got back to the federal building in Chelsea, Pauli Palson was secured in one of the interview rooms.

Entering the room, Pauli exploded, "Why am I here? I've been twiddling my thumbs for the past hour!"

"Tell me about Earl," Agent Bixby said.

"I've told Doyle everything; talk to him. He's sitting beside you."

"Perhaps no one has told you, Mr. Palson; you are being charged with a federal offense, intimidating a congressman," said Agent Bixby.

"I want my lawyer."

"Smart choice," said Bixby; "we will pick this up in the morning. Meanwhile, we have accommodations for you downstairs."

"What next?" asked Lieutenant Doyle.

60

"I'll let Palson stew in a cell overnight and then turn him loose in the morning with a promise that I'll get back to him. Now tell me about Carl Kitchener, CEO of NorthernLights."

"He's why I came to you in the first place. NorthernLights is located in Nashua. New Hampshire is outside my jurisdiction. As I told you, our investigation started with Gerontologisk Løft and our suspicion that its main ingredient, polymoxlymeth, was tainted. We followed the importation of polymoxlymeth from the port in Boston to the NorthernLights plant. We went so far as to put an undercover agent in the plant, Jimmy Anderson."

"Jimmy from Salt 'n Pepper?" asked Joyce.

"Yes. The Mayor engaged them to help the City's Department of Public Health investigate the deaths."

"Okay, tomorrow we visit Carl Kitchener, but first we should talk with Jimmy."

The next morning, I found Bixby and Doyle parking in front of Abe's Bookstore. Salt 'n Pepper had their office on the second floor. Parking on Charles Street is normally iffy, but Doyle took no notice of the parking signs.

Topping the stairs, Rosie greeted us, "Lieutenant Doyle, Uncle Jimmy said you'd be by this morning. Everyone is in the front office."

Agent Bixby, I think you know everyone," I said, pointing to Danny and Jimmy.

"Good morning, congressman," she said as she bent down to pat Maxi."

Straightening up, Joyce jokingly asked, "Has Maxi eaten any more bad guys this morning?"

After declining the offer of coffee, Joyce got down to business asking about NorthernLights and Carl Kitchener.

"Jimmy was able to confirm the transport of polymoxlymeth and its use in Gerontologisk Løft. He also had photos he'd taken on his cell of NorthernLights' accounting books," said Danny.

"How did you get those," Agent Bixby asked Jimmy.

"Let's just say I got them. You can see the markup. Industrial-grade polymoxlymeth costs one-tenth of what the medical-grade costs. My best guess suggests monthly illicit profits of thousands of dollars."

"Sam, you said NorthernLights was a subsidiary of ACME-Pharma," said Joyce. "As I recall, ACME-Pharma was found guilty of a situation that smells like what we have here. Any idea how involved ACME is in NorthernLights operations?"

"While I was there," Jimmy said, "this man," Jimmy held up his phone showing a man's picture, "visited Kitchener every Monday. I don't have his name or who he represents."

"Jimmy, can you put this all on paper and send it to me? But email me the photo now; it might be useful."

"Lieutenant, shall we get going? Kitchener, although he doesn't know it yet, is waiting for us. I'll call ahead and have local agents hold him in his office until we get there," said Joyce.

"Sam, if I had my druthers, I'd take Maxi with me to assist with interrogating Mr. Kitchener," Joyce said with a smile.

22 NortherLights

Carl Kitchener was a small, nervous man. The fact that he was met by FBI agents when he arrived at work that morning did nothing for his digestive system. By the time Agent Bixby and Lieutenant Doyle arrived, he was almost in a state of total collapse.

"Mr. Kitchener, I'm Agent Bixby, and have a few questions about NorthernLights, specifically Gerontologisk Løft. It has been linked to an increase in senior deaths in several States. The Boston Department of Public Health speculates that Gerontologisk Løft's main ingredient, polymoxlymeth, may be the cause. Recent polymoxlymeth shipments to your plant are believed to have been commercial-grade. Any comment?"

Kitchener, in a state of near panic, quips, "Impossible we only use the highest grade ingredients in our products. Look at our records. You will see we only order the best."

"Oh, we will," said Joyce. "We have a search warrant that allows us full access to your records."

"One more question," said Joyce, "what is your connection to ACME-Pharma?"

"That's public. Eight years ago, ACME acquired NorthernLights. We were having a cashflow problem and they stepped in to help. Since then, we have been an independent subsidiary," said Carl.

"And day-to-day operations, they have no say?" asked Agent Bixby.

"That's right, I manage NorthernLights," responded Kitchener.

The questioning continued for the rest of the morning as the FBI boxed up records and secured computer files.

"Once we get through this stuff," said Agent Bixby, "we'll be back."

That night, Carl Kitchener committed suicide, leaving a letter for Agent Bixby.

Upon hearing of Kitchener's suicide, Joyce had the letter opened and FAXed to her.

Agent Bixby,

I am so sorry about the deaths I caused. Yes, the polymoxlymeth we use is commercial-grade – we used it at ACAM-Pharma's direction. As I became aware of what was happening, I threatened Richard Cunningham, ACAM-Pharma's CEO, that I was going public. He laughed, saying I had no evidence to implicate him, and then threatened my family.

Eight years ago, shortly after ACME-Pharma acquired my company, Cunningham inserted his people into my plant ostensibly to improve production and lower costs. At first, there were notable improvements. Later, some of the changes made were legally questionable. A year after we acquired the license to produce Gerontologisk Løft from Hansen AG, ACAM-Pharma's experts suggested we could increase profits by switching to their supplier of polymoxlymeth, which costs only one-tenth the cost of Hansen AG's supplier. I should have known better, but I went along with it; profits were staggering.

*Your people took all the records I had in my office. If you contact my wife and ask for my private records, you will have the evidence **Cunningham** thought I did not have, more than enough to convict **him**.*

Tell my wife I love her and am sorry for taking the coward's way out. God forgive me.

Carl Kitchener

"Lieutenant are you ready for another trip to Nashua?" was the first thing she said when she called Doyle. She then read the letter.

By the time they arrived at the Kitchener home, the local police had finished, and the parish priest was with Mrs. Kitchener.

"Mrs. Kitchener, I'm so sorry to hear of your loss. I'm Agent Bixby with the FBI. I'm here to follow-up on some comments your husband made in his letter to me."

"It was you people who pushed Carl over the edge. Go away!" Mrs. Kitchener snapped.

Joyce handed her Carl's letter and said, "Mrs. Kitchener, please read this; they are your husband's last words."

As she read, she began to weep uncontrollably. The priest helped her to the sofa and attempted to calm her. After a few moments, Mrs. Kitchener said, "The records you want are in Carl's hunting lodge. Not many people know about the lodge; it's upstate on the Maine border."

23 FBI-Washington DC

ACME-Pharma's corporate headquarters is located in Delaware. They, in fact, produce nothing. They are a holding company. They buy small medical innovators, clinics, manufacturers of medical supplies, etc. Milk them for easy profits and then sell the carcasses. NorthernLights lasted longer than most in that NorthernLights provided a stream of profits from the sale of Gerontologisk Løft.

Given that ACME-Pharma's headquarters were outside the Boston FBI Field Office normal area and with the potential for political fallout, FBI Director Chris Raymond directed the case be reassigned to DC. Jacob Wainwright, the Crime Division Head, assigned Oscar Vicente as the lead agent.

Agent Bixby was still fuming when she arrived at National Airport. Taking the first taxi in the queue, she headed to the Hoover Building. To add insult to injury, the lobby guard would not let her enter until Jacob's office vouched for her.

Joyce was not a happy camper when she was ushered into the Director's office.

"Agent Bixby, thank you for coming to DC. We need to talk about ACME-Pharma. I expect you are royally pissed at having the lead reassigned to another agent. I've been there. Given the nature of the case and how I expect it to expand, we need a lead agent that has experience with other similar cases."

"I'm more than capable of handling this case!" responded Joyce.

"Your work history is outstanding. Bringing down Islamic terrorist cells, tracking IRA radicals. Well done. But you have little experience with offshore accounts, money laundering, and political bribery. I want you to work with Oscar as his backup. He will broaden your skill set."

Using the office intercom he asked his secretary, Ms. Maxwell, to send in Jacob.

"Agent Bixby, this is Jacob Wainwright, Head of the Crime Division. Agent Oscar Vicente is not available today; I believe Jacob has an in-briefing scheduled for tomorrow."

"Nine a.m. tomorrow," Jacob said. "I apologize for Agent Vicente's absence today, but it couldn't be helped."

"Where are you staying," the Director asked Agent Bixby.

"I don't know, I just got here."

"Let me recommend the Riggs Hotel. It's only a block away. We have an agreement with them to accept the Government per diem rate."

"Ms. Maxwell, would you mind taking Agent Bixby over to the Riggs, and given it is getting late, take the rest of the day off."

"Gee, thanks," Maxwell muttered. "A whole thirty minutes."

In the elevator going down to the parking level, Joyce said, "I'm sorry to be putting you out."

"No problem. Jacob and I are always bantering; he's a good boss. Besides, you got me out of the office a few minutes early. I tend to work late, and the Riggs is on my way home."

***

The following morning, as Joyce returned to the Hoover Building, walking the block and a half, she grabbed a coffee and a bite to eat at the Lincoln Waffle Shop. At the corner of 10th and E St. NW, she got her first full view of the Hoover Building, a brutal block of concrete. Not impressive.

"Entering the building, she was pleasantly surprised when the guard waved her through the turnstile and said, "Agent Bixby, Oscar is waiting for you in room 425. The elevator bank is to your left."

Oscar greeted her as she entered the conference room. Oscar was a small man, no more than five six and a hundred forty pounds, wet. Joyce thought he was either Cuban or Puerto Rican.

"I apologize for not being here yesterday," said Oscar. "I was just returning from Biloxi, wrapping up a cartel drug smuggling case. An interesting case. My inside man owns a Greek shipping company, just inherited a Biloxi-based coastal shipping company, and years ago shipped stolen cars to South America while smuggling illegals north. An interesting guy, but you'd best wear a protective cup when you deal with his wife, Magi."

Continuing, "I've been reviewing your case notes on ACME-Pharma, a good start." Pointing to the other man in the room, "This is Sydney Trocheck, a former mob money launderer, who has come over to the good side. He's traced NorthernLights illicit payments to Richard Cunningham's offshore account." Pointing again, "This lady, Susan Kenrick is an internet wiz, a hacker's hacker. She has dissected the account's transactions, in and out. NorthernLights is not the only company funding the account. Sydney and Susan are now attempting to track outflows that appear to be going to some prominent legislators."

"This might be bigger than I imagined," said Joyce. "Who are these other companies, and more importantly, the implicated politicians?"

"Not so fast," said Oscar. "We need to figure out how we are going to proceed. As Director Raymond told you, I am now the lead investigator on this case. How do you feel about that?"

"Pissed. You have more experience on these types of cases and obviously more resources, but I want to stay with it."

"As my backup?" asked Oscar.

"Yes."

For the next several hours the four reviewed data that had been collected and talked through several scenarios. Mid-afternoon, Sydney suggested he and Susan return to their office at the Quantico FBI Lab.

Oscar explained to Joyce that the two had a significant computer lab at Quantico and usually worked from there. "I have a few calls to make in the morning; after that would you like to visit Quantico?"

24 Findings

The following morning Oscar made two calls. The first to the Cincinnati field office where he asked the station chief to open a file on the Bigalow Techtronic's Company. The company's principal products were pacemakers, heart monitors, and defibrillators. They were having cash flow problems. ACME-Pharma recently bought a controlling share of the company.

The second call was to the Albuquerque field office with a similar request. The subject company in this case was M. Wellington, Inc. Wellington specialized in blood plasma. Again, ACME-Pharma recently acquired a controlling interest in the company.

As they drove down I-95 toward Quantico, Oscar explained that these two companies had surfaced like neon lights in the first cut of ACME's offshore account. "As we build our case, I want it to be broader than just NorthernLights," he said.

The FBI Laboratory was a definite improvement over the Hoover Building, thought Agent Bixby. The Laboratory was in a large, modern, multi-floor building in a park-like setting.

Jacob had a second office here. Sydney and Susan were waiting there when Oscar and Joyce arrived at eleven.

"Jacob loaned us his office for a bit," said Sydney as Susan brought to life the two large wall-mounted screens. On the first were transactions of deposits into Richard Cunningham's offshore account.

Most, but not all, transactions identified the originator. Deposits from Bigalow Techtronic's Company and M. Wellington, Inc. were sizable.

The second screen showed a list of withdrawals. Again, most recipients were identified, but not all. Notably, the largest withdrawals went to non-identified recipients. "Our current focus is identifying the non-identified recipients," said Sydney.

***

Back on Capitol Hill, Mike Spinelli was getting numerous calls from his constituents. Many wanted to know what he was doing about the growing ACME-Pharma scandal. The reports about the elderly who succumbed to holistic medicines were being overshadowed by a new medical emergency: tainted blood supplies. In recent days a few patients in New Mexico hospitals were diagnosed with exotic tropical blood diseases. The only commonality between them was that they all received blood transfusions, both whole blood and plasma.

An investigation by the State's health department found that whole blood managed by blood banks was clean, with no trace of contamination. This was not true for plasma. Two plasma packs were found to contain trace amounts of tropical diseases. Whole blood was collected in local blood drives. Plasma, on the other hand, was purchased. The State relied on three providers. The contaminated plasma packs were traced to M. Wellington, Inc., a company with a long history with the State.

The Head of New Mexico's Department of Public Health alerted public health departments in other States of New Mexico's findings as well as the Food and Drug Administration.

As the alert spread, several more cases of infected patients were identified. In several cases, those patients went on to infect others.

Sunday morning cable news had extensive coverage of the FDA's action for overseeing the nation's emergency blood supply. Commissioner Martha Madison had no answers.

Since M. Wellington, Inc. was a growing player in this scandal, Oscar directed the Albuquerque field office to dig into the company. The inquiry's finding was simple. Since **ACME-Pharma acquired control of M.** Wellington two years ago, blood has been collected from undocumented immigrants, providing substantial savings over screened collection sites. The CEO, when pressed, admitted the profits were sizable. He got a small cut; the rest went to **Richard Cunningham, ACAM-Pharma's CEO.**

Spinelli became more motivated to take action when he discovered his elderly aunt, his favorite aunt, was a victim of a tainted blood pack. She had recently undergone minor surgery and is now in the ICU, infected with Trypanosoma Cruzi, a pathogen common in Africa. He was chagrined when he learned M. Wellington was a subsidiary of ACME-Pharma. Wasn't it ACME-Pharma Sam wanted him to press the FDA to investigate?

25 Next

Several days later the Cincinnati field office got back to Oscar. "Agent Vicente," said the station chief, "we have an inside source at Bigalow who claims the company is using inferior circuit boards since ACME-Pharma acquired controlling interest. These circuit boards are coming from Shanghai. Previously, Bigalow purchased the boards from a company in Taiwan. My people followed up. Since ACME became a major holder of Bigalow's stock, there have been numerous deaths from undiagnosed heart problems. Several 911 rescue units have been reporting the failure of Bigalow defibrillators."

Oscar scheduled a meeting with Jacob later that morning to brief him on Bigalow. He also invited FDA Commissioner Martha Madison.

As Joyce later told me, it was not a pleasant meeting.

It started with Oscar asking Ms. Madison, "How much is ACME-Pharma paying you?"

Madison got all flustered, turned red, and started to leave the conference room when Jacob bellowed, "Sit-down! Three months ago the House subcommittee asked you about the homeopathic medicine Gerontologisk Løft produced by NorthernLights and its links to a rise in senior death rates. Today we find contaminated blood packs distributed by M. Wellington, Inc., a product monitored by the FDA. These blood packs have infected several patients with obscure tropical diseases. It has come to our attention that several 911 rescue units have been reporting the failure of Bigalow defibrillators. Can you tell us what

NorthernLights, M. Wellington, and Bigalow have in common Ms. Madison?"

Martha's lack of comment said volumes.

"I'll tell you Ms. Madison; they are all subsidiaries of ACME - Pharma. We are investigating ACME-Pharma's financial records, specifically their offshore account. There are several payments made to unspecified recipients. Our financial forensic team will soon be able to identify those recipients. I suspect one will be you."

"So, to repeat Agent Vicente's question, 'How much is ACME-Pharma paying you?'"

Martha Madison clammed up and quickly left the room.

***

Late that afternoon Agent Bixby made her way to the bowels of the Rayburn Building looking for Congressman Goodwin. Walking into his office, flashed her badge at Wanda; Wanda looked up, "What's that boy done now?

"Congressman, an FBI agent is here looking for you," yelled out Wanda.

"Agent Bixby, what brings you to my grotto," said Sam.

"Just wanted to see where you grow your mushrooms," responded Joyce. "I also wanted to update you since you were instrumental in getting us focused on ACME-Pharma. The FBI found a trove of records at Kitchener's lodge. They document ACME-Pharma's behind-the-scenes management of NorthernLights, detailing some of the shady practices."

"The pièce de resistance were the financial records. Profits from the sale of Gerontologisk Løft were deposited in Richard Cunningham's offshore account. We alerted the Treasury Department to these transactions. They have opened an investigation of both Cunningham and ACME-Pharma … a question about taxes."

"The FBI has formed a task force to dig into this growing scandal. I'm part of it." Joyce then went on to describe the morning meeting with Martha Madison.

"Now, why am I telling you this? You are linked to the FBI's investigation of ACME-Pharma, whether you want to be or not. In the next few months, as this plays out, your contemporaries on Capitol Hill are going to find one of the big donors to their political campaigns going down ... and a couple of them may go down with them."

"Now don't tell me," said Sam, "you want me to sit on this information."

"As a matter of fact, no. We would like you to let slip little tidbits here and there. We find that when people get nervous, they do dumb things," said Joyce. "Do it discreetly."

26   A Scare for Leadership

That Saturday the Intrepid Four met for our weekly brunch at the Metro 29 Diner. I repeated most of what Joyce shared with me and asked, "How do we use this information?"

"Since we are both from the southwest," said Susan Dillingham, "I occasionally talk with Mike. I know we have had a falling out with him, but he is being drawn back into ACME-Pharma's web. His aunt was infected with some exotic tropical disease. He's still on the Subcommittee on Health Care and Financial Services. I think he could be an asset."

"Do we know who the big recipients are of ACME-Pharma's campaign contributions?" asked Bob Mally.

"I'll ask Wanda to see what she can find," I said. "And in the meantime, what if I called Ron Abdow and get something into his Capitol Hill Gossip Column?"

When we left the diner, we had a plan. Susan would talk with Mike to encourage him to question the FDA's Commissioner. Bob and Premoday would quietly ask around to find other legislators with active concerns about ACME-Pharma, and I had my tasking.

The following Monday I found Wanda at her desk doing her nails. "Hard weekend congressman. Looks like you're the worse for wear."

"And good morning to you to Wanda. I spent the weekend researching ACME-Pharma. The more I learn, the worse they look. I have a question for you: can you find out which legislators got campaign contributions from ACME-Pharma and how much?"

"That's all in the public record," she said.

"I know, but how much was collected that was not reported? Are there any ongoing payments; stipends?"

"You want me to sneak around and be a spy?"

"Exactly. Pull in some favors. You know you love this stuff." And turning to my office, "Please don't disturb me for a while; I need to start drafting an article for Ron Abdow's column. And yes, I know I have a floor vote at eleven this morning."

I called Ron later that day and suggested we meet for lunch the next day. He wanted to know why; I told him I had some material for his gossip column.

We agreed to meet at the Hawk 'n' Dove, an upscale pub near Capitol Hill, after the lunch rush. He was waiting for me when I arrived. He had secured a booth in the back so we could talk privately. "Well congressman, what do you have for me?" I passed him a folder with my draft material. As he started to review it, I ordered a coffee and a Rubin sandwich.

Earlier this year Congressman Goodwin's wife was assaulted in their West Roxbury home. The two assailants were hospitalized with severe wounds: one on life support. They did not count on the Congressman's retired police dog Maxi.

The Boston police quickly identified NorthernLights CEO as sponsoring the attack. (Readers may recall my earlier posting about Congressman Goodwin's efforts to shine a light on NorthernLights and its parent holding company, ACME-Pharma.) NorthernLights CEO Carl Kitchener's suicide note confessed to hiring the hitmen, and here it takes a twist: hiring the hitmen was at Richard Cunningham, ACAM-Pharma's CEO, direction.

Assault on a congressional member, or family, is a federal offense. The FBI became involved in the case with Agent Bixby from the Boston Field Office being the lead investigator. Agent Bixby and the congressman have a work history. The congressman, a retired Boston police canine handler, was a private investigator prior to being elected to Congress. Collaboration between the two assisted law enforcement in outwitting ISIS terrorists in their attempt to poison NYC's water supply a couple of years ago.

The FBI Director relocated the task force to the Hoover Building because ACME-Pharma has a nationwide reach and possible political ramifications. He assigned it to a senior agent with extensive organized crime experience. Agent Bixby, relocated to Washington DC, remains on the case.

Congressman Goodwin and a small group of like-minded friends are assisting the FBI in their inquiry into ACME-Pharma.

After reading my draft, Ron said, "That's quite a story. Is any of it true?"

"Here are clippings from the Boston Globe and the NYT. Confirm it with them."

"And your interest in me posting this to my Capitol Hill Gossip Column?"

"Simple. I want to make people nervous. And before you ask, I'm doing what the FBI asked, shaking the bushes to see what falls out. If you post this to your column, I'll keep you on the inside track for breaking news," I said.

27 Money

Wanda didn't disappoint. Within a matter of days, she had a detailed list of ACME-Pharma's campaign contributions going back several years. I was not surprised to see the House Speaker and the Majority Whip as being the top recipients of ACME's generosity, each receiving millions over past elections. The number of committee chairmen receiving large donations was a little surprising. Even Congressman Smyth received a few dollars. What was surprising was that similar amounts had been contributed to the opposition.

"This is great Wanda. Any problem getting it?" I asked.

"No, all public records, kept by the House clerk. Now this," she said as she handed me another folder, "was collected from some confidential sources."

I was spellbound looking through the second folder. It listed several prominent congressional members allegedly receiving periodic payments from ACME-Pharma. "How in heaven's name did you get this information? Is it reliable?"

"I got it from the support staff. You know, those people hanging around in the background keeping things running – like me. Most the hotshots have loose lips around their office staff. As for being reliable, much of it is undoubtedly blowhards bragging. But there is probably some truth here. Don't discount it all."

I gave Agent Bixby a call and suggested we meet that evening. I had some goodies for her. She suggested a sports bar not far from the Hoover Building, the *Penn Social* at seven,

I took the Metro. On the map, the Gallery Place Metro stop was near the bar. I got turned around and was late getting there. I found Agent Bixby and another person sitting at one of those tall round tables in the middle of the room. I mounted the free stool he pushed out to me.

"I hope you don't mind that I brought Oscar," said Joyce. "Agent Vicente is the lead agent on our investigation."

"Ron Abdow's recent post in his gossip column has my boss, spun up. "I don't suppose you had anything to do with it?" Oscar said with a half-smile.

"Agent Bixby suggested I rattle some cages," I replied. "Since its publication, I've been getting mixed reactions on the Hill."

"Did your dog really put the two assailants in the hospital?" asked Oscar.

Not waiting for my reply, Joyce jumped in recounting Maxi's integration technique. "I've seen her straddling a perp, snarling inches from his face, as he spilled his guts."

"Carol is Maxi's adopted mother. If you threaten her, Maxi will take you down. When the guy hit Carol, Maxi went nuts. He's alive today only because Carol pulled her off and applied pressure to his throat which Maxi was using as a chew toy," I said.

"Getting back on topic," I continued, "at Joyce's suggestion, I've collected a little information on ACME's campaign contributions. Most of this information is readily available; you probably already have it. But if you look at the second folder there is a list of contributions allegedly made under the table and not reported. I doubt if you have that information. But now for the icing on the cake, the third folder identifies two House members supposedly receiving monthly payments."

As Joyce looked over the material she's asking, "How did you get this? Is it reliable?"

"You've met my receptionist. Wanda has an intelligence network that you can only dream of. The Hill's support staff outlasts most politicians and, regardless of affiliation, backs each other up."

As Oscar continues to study the lists, he finally says, "Two names jump out. Sizable campaign contributions, both over and under the table, to House Speaker Mansfield and the House Majority Whip, Richards. Also alleged monthly payments to Mansfield. Sam, do you think these men are dirty?" he asked, looking at me.

"Both do their best to deflect any scrutiny of ACME-Pharma. So yes, I think it's probable they are dirty."

"Oscar," said Joyce, "can Sydney trace some of the unknown transfers assuming Mansfield is the recipient?"

***

Now having a possible target, Sydney traced the periodic payments from Richard Cunningham's offshore account to the Riggs Bank.

Sydney had to get Susan Kenrick's help to tease out the account owner's name, George Mansfield.

Susan, an internet sleuth, was one of the reasons Sydney turned on the mob. That and a prison stay if he didn't cooperate with the Feds. But the short of it was, Sydney and Susan were Jacob's secret weapon in fighting organized crime.

28 A Proposal

Once Sydney and Susan solved the financial puzzle, things began to happen. The first casualty was Martha Madison, the FDA Commissioner. She was charged with accepting bribes to overlook ACME-Pharma's growing list of the illegal practices of their subsidiaries.

Oscar had ACME-Pharma's CEO, Richard Cunningham, brought in for questioning. No direct link could tie him to the offshore account other than Carl Kitchener's suicide note. The connection Sydney established, i.e., the flow of funds, could not be used in court; let's just say the methods used were reminiscent of Sydney's time with the mob.

FBI Director Chris Raymond directed Jacob to delay actions against House Speaker Mansfield and House Majority Whip Richards until after the upcoming presidential election, now nine months away.

Despite the FBI's delay, rumors swirled around Capitol Hill. There was a growing movement to remove Mansfield from his Speaker's position and replace him with Congressman Roy Danials.

Thursday of that week Premoday Khakha contacted the other three members of the Intrepid Four, encouraging their attendance at Saturday's brunch. He was bringing a surprise visitor. Premoday was the least vocal of our group; I was intrigued.

That Saturday the three of us arrived early at the Metro 29 Diner. We were on our second cup of coffee when Premoday ushered in his guest. As Premoday was making introductions, it was all we could do to mask our surprised looks. Premoday's guest was Tim Clark, the House Minority Leader.

As they pulled up chairs, Tim said, "The looks on your faces are priceless. You'd think the devil himself arrived."

"I've been talking with Congressman Clark the past few days feeling out a possible course of action for us," said Premoday. "As you know, Mansfield has been stonewalling our actions directed at the FDA. We all have promised our constituents back home that we have their backs. You also know Mansfield, and his lackey Richards have pending FBI cases against them for allegedly accepting bribes to protect ACME-Pharm,".

Susan, growing interested in this conversation, responded. "Yes, we all know that. So, what is your proposal? How does the House Minority Leader fit in?"

"Let me respond," said Clark as he waved Premoday down. "What I'm suggesting is somewhat unorthodox. I'm suggesting the four of you step back from the Democratic Party and declare yourselves as Independents. You can still caucus with the Party, but your vote would be less certain. The Ethics Committee will be seeking to censor Mansfield and Richards next week. Your four votes will give us two hundred twenty, enough to pass the resolution."

"Short of political suicide," said Bob, "why would we do that?"

"My members will support a full investigation of the FDA, ACME-Pharma, and the alleged bribes."

"I know you find this to be a radical proposal. Talk it over. Premoday can get back to me Monday," Clark said as he got up to leave. "Thank you for your time."

The four of us sat there with our own thoughts.

"I like it," I finally said. "My loyalty is to my constituents, not the Party. This gives us what we've been looking for, a path to justice."

Susan and Premoday were in agreement. Bob, on the other hand, was not.

"Sam, we know you don't plan to seek a second term. And you two, pointing to Susan and Premoday, are in districts that support the candidate over the Party. I plan to run for a second term and my district is 'blue.' If I did this, I would not survive."

On Monday Premoday told Clark he had three of the four votes. Two hundred and nineteen votes would win the day. As he passed on this information, there were three defections from the left side of the aisle, three new Independent members in the House.

House Speaker Mansfield was furious but there was nothing he could do. Later that week the Ethics Committee voted to censure Mansfield and Richards. The full House vote resulted in two hundred eighteen votes in support. One Republican missed the vote due to a health issue, but two hundred eighteen votes were enough to pass the resolution. Mansfield became the first sitting Speaker of the House censured by the House.

28 Just Deserts

Robert Brisco (D-KS) introduced legislation to decriminalize marijuana, Nationwide. The bill was drafted by ACME-Pharma's attorneys but given the disarray on the left side of the aisle, it got no traction. Repeated phone calls by ACME-Pharma went unanswered.

Richard Cunningham was cursing his phone on his third attempt to get Mansfield on the line. His lead attorney, in the office with him, tried to placate him and said, "Bob, Mansfield is facing an internal revolt. He can't push our bill forward; he'd have no support. I suggest we ask Brisco to pull back our proposed legislation and reintroduce it after the election."

"You're right. If we push too hard now, the bill may die for good. If the rumors I've been hearing are true, we may need to buy a new House Speaker. Have your people look into possible candidates."

"I have three greedy candidates; Robert Brisco is one. We can discuss it after your field trip. Where are you going again?" asked Mathew.

"To get the working half of the bill we just decided to delay. The Kickapoo's, yes, a real Indian tribe located in the northeast corner of Kansas, has a small marijuana operations supplying tribal needs. I'm going to buy into it and expand it to supply the Midwest, Chicago to Dallas. So you best get Brisco's butt in gear."

"Bob, that market is saturated," said Mathew. "It will be a scramble to get a decent profit."

"That's the beauty of it. The Kickapoo's weed is known to be high quality. I'm going to bring trash weed from Mexico and mix it in. I should be able to sell it for a couple of years at a high profit before we lose the market and I dump the operation. Your job is to get that bill passed next year."

Two days later Richard Cunningham, in ACME-Phama's corporate jet landed at the Topeka regional airport. The Kickapoo reservation was forty miles north of Topeka. Mathew had arranged for an SUV to be waiting for Cunningham.

At the reservation, Cunningham was met by Chief Toby Whitetail.

The Chief took Cunningham on a tour of the operation, the building, the machinery, and the fields. Toby had refreshments available on the edge of the field where the cannabis was grown. Sitting at a card table with an adult beverage, Toby was saying, "It's the soil here that gives us such primo weed."

Conningham's cell started vibrating. Looking at the screen he saw it was his attorney, Mathew. "Excuse me, I have to take this."

Walking to the edge of the field, Mathew starts with an excited voice, "The Feds are here. They have a warrant for your arrest for tax evasion. I told you to pay tax on those deposits in the Caribbean."

"How the hell did they find those?" fumed Cunningham.

"I don't know, but I suggest you disappear. Your secretary just told the FBI where you are."

"Shit, my plane is an hour away. See if you can delay them; give me time to get airborne."

Returning to the group, Cunningham excused himself, claiming it was a family emergency. Rushing to the SUV, he ordered the driver to take him back to the airport. "There's a hundred-dollar tip if I'm there in a half hour."

The SUV is speeding south, ignoring all traffic signs. As it ran a red light, it was broadsided by a farm truck trying to make up some time.

The SUV, seriously damaged on the passenger side, rolled into the ditch running alongside the road. The farmhands, in broken English, called 911 to report the accident.

Twenty minutes later the county rescue vehicle arrived. The SUV driver, other than some scrapes, was uninjured. Cunningham, on the other hand, was unconscious and losing blood. When the team extracted him from the wreck it was quickly decided to take him to the nearest medical facility, the hospital on the Kickapoo reservation. This hospital is best described as a large clinic.

After he regained consciousness and was medically stabilized, two FBI agents entered his hospital room and announced he was under arrest.

One of the agents had been following the case against ACME-Pharma. His cousin, Bob Mally, had been keeping the family up to date on House shenanigans.

"Mr. Conningham," the agent said. "You're lucky. You lost a lot of blood. The hospital couldn't match your blood type but had a small supply of blood plasma available. Earlier this year, Wellington issued a recall for all the plasma it sold, but this hospital's supply was overlooked. They pumped two packs into you."

29 Post Election

It was late November and I found myself sitting in the Metro 29 dinner waiting for our small group to assemble. All had abandoned Capitol Hill to get in the final weeks of campaigning. Susan was the first to arrive. She was upbeat, obviously winning a second term. Bob and Premoday wandered in a few minutes later, high-fiving each other. Mike had not survived the election.

"I see congratulations are in order," I said.

"And you?" Bob asked.

You're stuck with me for another two years.

"You said you weren't running again," said Susan. "Congratulations are in order … I think."

"I didn't plan to. Mayor O'Brien got to my wife and convinced her I was doing a good job. I ran as an Independent and got 62 percent of the vote in one of Boston's bluest districts."

"Mansfield lost his bid for reelection. He got fewer votes than even his opposition expected. He's out," said Premoday "as is his sidekick, Richards."

Election results give the Democrats a slight edge, two hundred seventeen clean wins. There are seven contests still unresolved, but the bet is three will go to the Democrats.

"If I'm counting right, we four Independents can swing the House either way."

"Let's keep our powder dry," said Susan. "I suspect both sides will make nice to us."

"Changing topics," Bob said; "you know ACME-Pharma's CEO was taken into custody. My cousin made the arrest. Cunningham was trying to cut a deal with the Kickapoo Indian tribe to market marijuana when he got word the FBI was closing in on him. He made a run for his plane, in his haste was in a vehicle accident and seriously injured. The closest medical facility was the hospital on the Kickapoo reservation. He needed a blood transfusion. The hospital couldn't match his blood type but had a small supply of blood plasma available ... M. Wellington's plasma packs. Later when told, he knew there was a chance he'd contract some tropical disease from the plasma. He spent the next several weeks more worried about 'beriberi' than prison."

***

I had been offered a sunny office on the 4th floor. After thinking about it, I opted to stay in the basement; Wanda wouldn't move upstairs, and she was worth more than any view.

That January the new prospective House Speaker, Congressman Roy Danials from Massachusetts, called all newly elected House members together, all four hundred thirty-five of us. To the left were two hundred seventeen and to the right two hundred fourteen. And four Independents, caucusing with the left, were sitting in the middle.

After the swearing-in oath was administered, House members were released to find their new offices. Congressman Danials, a veteran of the House, invited me to his office that afternoon to discuss some new legislation he was considering. I agreed, saying I'd have one of my fellow Independents with me. He nodded his agreement; what else could he do?

"Sam, I see you couldn't get enough of this place," Wanda said chucking. "What was it that kept you in the basement, my girlish figure?"

"Your pleasant personality I retorted."

Later that afternoon Susan and I made our way to Mansfield's old office. Daniels was in the process of moving in.

"Thanks for coming," he said as he waved us to the outer office. "The paint is still drying in there; we can use the nook over here to talk.

"Phillis, can you get our guests some coffee or tea," he said looking at us.

After coffee was served and we were comfortably settled, Danials asked, "What are your major objectives for this session?"

Susan and I looked at each other before I responded, "The welfare of our constituents."

"That's rather broad isn't it," said the would be Speaker.

Those were the exact words we got from the House Minority Leader," said Susan.

END

www.ingramcontent.com/pod-product-compliance
Lightning Source LLC
Chambersburg PA
CBHW020631130626
46552CB00003B/1180